Richard Henry Stoddard

Nathaniel Hawthorne

Antigonos

Richard Henry Stoddard

Nathaniel Hawthorne

Reprint of the original, first published in 1879.

1st Edition 2024 | ISBN: 978-3-38800-508-9

Antigonos Verlag is an imprint of Outlook Verlagsgesellschaft mbH.

Verlag (Publisher): Outlook Verlag GmbH, Zeilweg 44, 60439 Frankfurt, Deutschland, info@outlook-verlag.de
Vertretungsberechtigt (Authorized to represent): E. Roepke, Zeilweg 44, 60439 Frankfurt, Deutschland
Druck (Print): Libri Plureos GmbH, Friedensallee 273, 22763 Hamburg, Deutschland

NATHANIEL HAWTHORNE

BY

RICHARD HENRY STODDARD

———

NEW YORK
CHARLES SCRIBNER'S SONS
1879
—

Trow's
Printing and Bookbinding Company,
201-213 East Twelfth Street,
New York.

NATHANIEL HAWTHORNE.

THE family name of Nathaniel Hawthorne was spelled Hathorne until it was changed by him in early manhood to its present form. The head of the American branch of the family, William Hathorne, of Wilton, Wiltshire, England, emigrated with Winthrop and his company, and arrived at Salem Bay, Mass., June 12, 1630. He had grants of land at Dorchester, where he resided for upwards of six years, when he was persuaded to remove to Salem by the tender of further grants of land there, it being considered a public benefit that he should become an inhabitant of that town. He represented his fellow-townsmen in the legislature, and served them in a military capacity as a captain in the first regular troop organized in Salem, which he led to victory through an Indian campaign in Maine. Originally a determined " Sepa-

ratist," and opposed to compulsion for conscience
he signalized himself when a magistrate by the
active part which he took in the Quaker persecu-
tions of the time (1657–62), going so far on one
occasion as to order the whipping of Anne Cole-
man and four other Friends through Salem,
Boston, and Dedham.   He died, an old man,
in the odor of sanctity, and left a good prop-
erty to his son John, who inherited his father's
capacity and intolerance, and was in turn a
legislator, a magistrate, a soldier, and a bit-
ter persecutor of witches.   Before the death
of Justice Hathorne in 1717, the destiny of
the family suffered a sea-change, and they be-
gan to be noted as mariners.   One of these
seafaring Hathornes figured in the Revolution
as a privateer, who had the good fortune to es-
cape from a British prison-ship ; and another,
Captain Daniel Hathorne, has left his mark on
early American ballad-lore.   He too was a
privateer, commander of the brig " Fair American," which, cruising off the coast of Portugal,
fell in with a British scow laden with troops
for General Howe, which scow the bold Hathorne and his valiant crew at once engaged,
and fought for over an hour, until the van-

quished enemy was glad to cut the Yankee grapplings and quickly bear away. The last of the Hathornes with whom we are concerned was a son of this sturdy old privateer, Nathaniel Hathorne. He was born in 1776, and about the beginning of the present century married Miss Elizabeth Clarke Manning, a daughter of Richard Manning of Salem, whose ancestors emigrated to America about fifty years after the arrival of William Hathorne. Young Nathaniel took his hereditary place before the mast, passed from the forecastle to the cabin, made voyages to the East and West Indies, Brazil, and Africa, and finally died of fever at Surinam, in the spring of 1808. He was the father of three children, the second of whom, Nathaniel, was born at Salem, July 4, 1804.

After the death of her husband Mrs. Hathorne removed to the house of her father with her little family of children. Of the boyhood of Nathaniel no particulars have reached us, except that he was fond of taking long walks alone, and that he used to declare to his mother that he would go to sea some time, and would never return. Among the books that he is known to have read as a child were Shakespeare,

Milton, Pope, and Thomson, *The Castle of Indolence* being an especial favorite. In the autumn of 1818 his mother removed to Raymond, a town in Cumberland county, Maine, where his uncle, Richard Manning, had built a large and ambitious dwelling. Here the lad resumed his solitary walks, exchanging the narrow streets of Salem for the boundless, primeval wilderness, and its sluggish harbor for the fresh, bright waters of Sebago Lake. He roamed the woods by day, with his gun and rod, and in the moonlight nights of winter skated upon the lake alone till midnight. When he found himself away from home, and wearied with his exercise, he took refuge in a log cabin, where half a tree would be burning upon the hearth. He had by this time acquired a taste for writing, that showed itself in a little blank-book, in which he jotted down his woodland adventures and feelings, and which was remarkable for minute observation and nice perception of nature.

After a year's residence at Raymond, Nathaniel returned to Salem in order to prepare for college. He amused himself by publishing a manuscript periodical, which he called the *Spectator*, and which displayed considerable vivacity and talent. He speculated upon the profession that he would follow, with a sort of prophetic insight into his future. "I do not want to be a doctor and live by men's diseases," he wrote to his mother, "nor a minister to live by their sins, nor a lawyer and live by their quarrels. So, I don't see that there is anything left for me but to be an author. How would you like some day to see a whole shelf full of books, written by your son, with ' Hawthorne's Works' printed on their backs ?"

Nathaniel entered Bowdoin College, Brunswick, Maine, in the autumn of 1821, where he became acquainted with two students who were destined to distinction—Henry W. Longfellow and Franklin Pierce. He was an excellent classical scholar, his Latin compositions, even in his freshman year, being remarkable for their elegance, while his Greek (which was less) was good. He made graceful translations from the Roman poets, and wrote several English poems which were creditable to him. After his graduation, three years later, he returned to Salem, and to a life of isolation. He devoted his mornings to study, his afternoons to writing, and his evenings to long walks along the rocky

coast.   He was scarcely known by sight to his
townsmen, and he held so little communication
with the members of his own family that his
meals were frequently left at his locked door.
He wrote largely, but destroyed many of his
manuscripts, his taste was so difficult to please.
He thought well enough, however, of one of
his compositions to print it anonymously in
1828.   A crude melodramatic story, entitled
Fanshawe it was unworthy even of his immature powers, and should never have been
rescued from the oblivion which speedily overtook it.   The name of Nathaniel Hawthorne
finally became known to his countrymen as a
writer in *The Token*, a holiday annual which was
commenced in 1828 by Mr. S. G. Goodrich
(better known as " Peter Parley "), by whom
it was conducted for fourteen years.   This forgotten publication numbered among its contributors most of the prominent American
writers of the time, none of whom appear to
have added to their reputation in its pages, except the least popular of all—Hawthorne, who
was for years the obscurest man of letters in
America, though he gradually made admirers
in a quiet way.   His first public recognition

came from England, where his genius was dis-
covered in 1835 by the late Henry F. Chorley,
one of the editors of the *Athenæum*, in which
he copied three of Hawthorne's most character-
istic papers from *The Token*. He had but
little encouragement to continue in literature,
for Mr. Goodrich was so much more a publisher
than an author that he paid him wretchedly for
his contributions, and still more wretchedly for
his work upon an *American Magazine of Use-
ful and Entertaining Knowledge*, which he persuaded him to edit. This author-publisher consented, however, at a later period (1837) to
bring out a collection of Hawthorne's writings
under the title of *Twice-told Tales*. A mod-
erate edition was got rid of, but the great body
of the reading public ignored the book alto-
gether. It was generously reviewed in the *North
American Review* by his college friend Longfellow, who said it came from the hand of a
man of genius, and praised it for the exceeding
beauty of its style, which was as clear as run-
ning waters.

The want of pecuniary success which had so
far attended his authorship led Hawthorne to
accept a situation which was tendered him by

Mr. George Bancroft, the historian, collector of the port of Boston under the Democratic rule of President Van Buren. He was appointed a weigher in the custom-house at a salary of about $1,200 a year, and entered upon the duties of his office, which consisted for the most part in measuring coal, salt, and other bulky commodities on foreign vessels. It was irksome employment, but faithfully performed for two years, when he was superseded through a change in the national administration. Master of himself once more, he returned to Salem, where he remained until the spring of 1841, when he wrote a collection of children's stories entitled *Grandfather's Chair*, and joined an industrial association at West Roxbury, Mass. Brook Farm, as it was called, was a social Utopia, composed of a number of advanced thinkers, whose object was so to distribute manual labor as to give its members time for intellectual culture. The scheme worked admirably—on paper, but it was suited neither to the temperament nor the taste of Hawthorne, and after trying it patiently for nearly a year he returned to the everyday life of mankind.

One of Hawthorne's earliest admirers was

Miss Sophia Peabody, a lady of Salem, whom he married in the summer of 1842. He made himself a new home in an old manse, at Concord, Mass., situated on historic ground, in sight of an old revolutionary battle-field, and devoted himself diligently to literature. He was known to the few by his *Twice-told Tales*, and to the many by his papers in the *Democratic Review*. He published in 1842 a second portion of *Grandfather's Chair*, and in 1845 a second volume of *Twice-told Tales*. He edited, during the latter year, the *African Journals* of Horatio Bridge, an officer of the navy, who had been at college with him ; and in the following year he published in two volumes a collection of his later writings, under the title of *Mosses from an Old Manse*.

After a residence of nearly four years at Concord, Hawthorne returned to Salem, having been appointed surveyor of the custom-house of that port by a new Democratic administration. He filled the duties of this position until the incoming of the Whig administration again led to his retirement. He seems to have written little during his official term, but, as he had leisure enough and to spare, he read much, and pondered over subjects for future stories. His next work, *The Scarlet Letter*, which was begun after his removal from the custom-house, was published in 1850. If there had been any doubt of his genius before, it was settled forever by this powerful romance.

Shortly after the publication of *The Scarlet Letter* Hawthorne removed from Salem to Lenox, Berkshire, Mass., where he wrote *The House of the Seven Gables* (1851) and *The Wonder-Book* (1851). From Lenox he removed to West Newton, near Boston, Mass., where he wrote *The Blithedale Romance* (1852) and *The Snow Image and other Twice-told Tales* (1852). In the spring of 1852 he removed back to Concord, where he purchased an old house which he called The Wayside, and where he wrote a *Life of Franklin Pierce* (1852) and *Tanglewood Tales* (1853). Mr. Pierce was the Democratic candidate for the presidency, and it was only at his urgent solicitation that Hawthorne consented to become his biographer. He declared that he would accept no office in case he were elected, lest it might compromise him, but his friends gave him such weighty reasons for reconsidering his decision that he accepted the consulate at Liverpool, which was understood to be one of the best gifts at the disposal of the President.

Hawthorne departed for Europe in the summer of 1853, and returned to the United States in the summer of 1860. Of the seven years which he passed in Europe five were spent in attending to the duties of his consulate at Liverpool, and in little journeys to Scotland, the Lakes, and elsewhere, and the remaining two in France and Italy. They were quiet and uneventful, colored by observation and reflection, as his note-books show, but productive of only one elaborate work, *The Marble Faun*, which he sketched out during his residence in Italy, and rewrote and prepared for the press at Leamington, England, whence it was dispatched to America and published in 1860.

Hawthorne took up his abode at The Wayside, not much richer than when he left it, and sat down at his desk once more with a heavy heart. He was surrounded by the throes of a great civil war, and the political party with which he had always acted was under a cloud. His friend ex-President Pierce was stigmatized as a traitor, and when Hawthorne dedicated his next book to him—a volume of English impressions entitled *Our Old Home* (1863)—it was at the risk of his own popularity. His pen was soon to be laid aside forever; for, with the exception of the unfinished story of *Septimius Felton*, which was published after his death by his daughter Una (1872), and the fragment of *The Dolliver Romance*, the beginning of which was published in the *Atlantic Monthly* in July, 1864, he wrote no more. His health gradually declined; his hair grew white as snow, and the once stalwart figure that in early manhood flashed along the airy cliffs and glittering sands sauntered idly on the little hill behind his house. In the beginning of April, 1864, he made a short southern tour with his publisher Mr. William D. Ticknor, and was benefited by the change of scene until he reached Philadelphia, where he was shocked by the sudden death of Mr. Ticknor. He returned to The Wayside, and after a short season of rest joined his friend ex-President Pierce. He died at Plymouth, New Hampshire, on May 19, 1864, and five days later was buried at Sleepy Hollow, a beautiful cemetery at Concord, where he used to walk under the pines when he was living at the Old Manse, and where his ashes moulder under a simple stone, inscribed with the single word " Hawthorne."

The writings of Hawthorne are marked by subtle imagination, curious power of analysis, and exquisite purity of diction. He studied exceptional developments of character, and was fond of exploring secret crypts of emotion. His shorter stories are remarkable for originality and suggestiveness, and his larger ones are as absolute creations as *Hamlet* or *Undine*. Lacking the accomplishment of verse, he was in the highest sense a poet. His work is pervaded by a manly personality, and by an almost feminine delicacy and gentleness. He inherited the gravity of his Puritan ancestors without their superstition, and learned in his solitary meditations a knowledge of the night-side of life which would have filled them with suspicion. A profound anatomist of the heart, he was singularly free from morbidness, and in his darkest speculations concerning evil was robustly right-minded. He worshipped conscience with his intellectual as well as his moral nature; it is supreme in all he wrote. Besides these mental traits, he possessed the literary quality of style—a grace, a charm, a perfection of language which no other American writer ever possessed in the same degree, and which places him among the great masters of English prose.